The S☀lar Lantern

Ishan Mahapatra

notionpress
.com

INDIA · SINGAPORE · MALAYSIA

ISBN 979-8-89984-868-1

Preface

When my son, Ishan, first told me he wanted to write about our summer at Verdelia, I thought it would be a simple travel diary—maybe a few sketches of pine trees and a recollection of the family dinners we shared. What emerged instead was a deeply thoughtful and evocative account of a journey far more profound than any of us had anticipated.

Through a child's eyes—curious, observant and refreshingly honest—I watched Ishan reflect on the small but significant moments that unfolded during those few days in the hills. From the warm glow of a solar lantern at the Whispering Pines Retreat to conversations about sustainable feasts and the sobering realities of conflict, he captured not only scenes but also values. These chapters are not just memories; they are quiet lessons in sustainability, empathy and peace.

What touched me the most as a father was not just Ishan's grasp of environmental responsibility or his questions about war and peace, but his growing awareness of our shared role in shaping a better world. His words reminded me of the incredible power children hold—not just as future leaders, but as present-day beacons of thought and change.

This book is his voice. But it is also, in a way, a mirror—reflecting the questions we all ought to be asking, the choices we must begin to make, and the gentler, greener path we could walk together.

I share this with great pride. Not as a literary critic. Not even just as a parent. But as someone who truly believes that even the smallest stories, told with sincerity, can light the way—much like the solar lanterns that first sparked his imagination.

– Prasun Mahapatra

Contents

Chapter 1
Verdelia

The best part of school exams is the holidays that come after. They give us a much needed break. My family often feels confined in the busy city's concrete jungle. We always look forward to escaping. This year, during my summer vacation, we chose to visit the serene hill station of Verdelia.

We chose to stay at the Whispering Pines Retreat. The retreat was nestled among rolling hills and lush greenery. It felt like a peaceful haven. Colourful flowers lined the paths. Tall pine trees gently swayed in the breeze. The air was crisp and fresh.

In the mornings, we woke up to the sound of birds chirping. The views of mist covered mountains were stunning. Surrounded by the serenity of nature it was the perfect escape from the city's chaos.

During our first night's dinner at the Whispering Pines Retreat, the serene ambience was abruptly interrupted by a power outage. Swiftly my Mom reached into her magical vanity bag, searching for torches to illuminate our surroundings in the sudden darkness.

I was puzzled and inquired,"Dad, why do we need these?"

My Dad explained,"Sometimes, unforeseen events occur, and it's good to be prepared.

These will help us see in the dark until the power comes back on."

As my Mom delved into her bag, the Whispering Pines Retreat staff,seemingly one step ahead, moved with urgency. As they entered the room I saw them carrying lanterns in their hands. The flickering shadows of the staff danced on the walls of the dining room. The light of the lanterns gracefully filled the dimly lit space with a bright and sustainable glow.

I was captivated by the sight and remarked, "Dad, what are those lanterns? They're shining so brightly but look different from the lanterns I have seen anywhere else."

My Dad observed the glow. He leaned in and explained, "Sam, those lanterns are special. They're powered by the Sun. It's a sustainable way to light up the place without using regular electricity."

The dinner hall was filled with the delicious aroma of delicacies. As the glow of the solar lanterns from the Whispering Pines Retreat illuminated the room I was yet to understand then how the events in my life for the following days would lead me to a path of a greener future.

Unless someone like
'YOU'
cares a whole awful lot
Nothing is going to get
better, it's not. The Lorax

Chapter 2
A Sustainable Feast

I was not sure as to how long I slept but next day the crisp morning air in Verdelia stirred me from my peaceful slumber at the Whispering Pines Retreat.

As the memories of the previous night's dinner slowly crept back into my consciousness, I couldn't shake off the sense of curiosity that lingered. The dishes, the flavours and Dad's words about the solar lantern replayed in my mind like a pleasant melody.

Eager to hear more, as I climbed up the stairs the aroma of the breakfast welcomed me. Finding Dad sipping his morning tea on the terrace, I could not contain my questions any longer.

With curiosity bubbling over I asked,"Dad, last night's dinner was different!"

Dad smiled. He recognized the intrigue in my eyes and replied, "Ah, you're curious, I see. I agree the dinner we had last night was different in many ways and that's because what we had indulged in was a sustainable feast."

With double curiosity I asked, "A sustainable feast! "

Dad assumed I knew nothing of sustainable feast. He explained, "Well, a sustainable feast is about making choices that are good for the environment. It means picking foods that are grown locally, using minimal packaging and supporting ethical farming practices."

I inquired, "But, why did we have a sustainable feast last night? And, why was the food different?"

As I joined him at the table, Dad, with a twinkle in his eyes, began to unravel the tale of our sustainable dinner. He explained, "Sam, the Whispering Pines Retreat is not just a beautiful place to stay, it's a place that cares about the planet. The chef here prioritizes ingredients that are good for the environment, like locally sourced vegetables and seafood caught in sustainable ways."

I nodded and started to connect the dots. I asked, "That's why the dishes had those colourful vegetables and tasted so fresh?"

Dad chuckled and said, "Exactly! And when we choose locally sourced ingredients, it not only supports local farmers but also reduces the need to transport food over long distances. This, in turn, helps lower emissions and pollution that can harm the environment. Vehicles, needed to transport and carry those vegetables to the markets and kitchens, need to travel less and thereby emit less smoke and thus pollute the environment lesser."

I was genuinely puzzled. I asked,"But why don't we always eat sustainably? Why do some people eat things that are not good for the environment?"

Dad patted my shoulder, appreciating my thoughtful questions. He said,"Well Sam, not everyone has the same access to sustainable options. Sometimes people might not be aware of the impact of their choices. It's about awareness and making the best choices we can with the information we have."

As we enjoyed our breakfast, I felt a newfound sense of responsibility settling within me. The sustainable feast was not a one time event but a step toward a lifestyle that considered the well-being of the planet in every meal.

In the days that followed, our family continued to explore Verdelia. Every meal became an opportunity to make sustainable choices. Each bite became a celebration of our commitment to a healthier and happier planet. With every step, the Whispering Pines Retreat became not just a temporary escape but a guide toward a more sustainable way of living.

Chapter 3
A Waging War

The day slowly unfolded. As dusk settled over the blue hills of Verdelia, I found Dad on the porch of the Whispering Pines Retreat. He was deeply absorbed in the evening edition of the Hillview Herald.

The newspaper rustled in his hands as he read through the day's news. The hotel's park had become my playground. I happily spent my time on the seesaw, swing and merry-go-round. Then a headline in the Hillview Herald caught my eyes. "A Tale of a Waging War Between the Nations of Lumaria and Crestoria."

I tried to play beneath the ancient trees. However, the unsettling news gripped my thoughts. The peaceful setting of Verdelia felt worlds apart from the conflicts described in the newspaper.

I called out, "Dad, why do countries go to war? It seems like all they get is destruction and sadness."

Dad folded the newspaper and then joined me on the park bench. He added, "Sam, wars cause human suffering and environmental damage. The air becomes polluted with harmful gases. The lives of ordinary people are devastated. It's a complex issue. We hope for a world where diplomacy and understanding can replace battles!"

That night, as the Sun dipped below the horizon, my mind was filled with a warm question and wandered back to the turmoil in the Hillview Herald. I imagined the beautiful hills of Verdelia being scarred. I imagined the air turning toxic. The peaceful Whispering Pines Retreat and Verdelia seemed to stand in stark contrast to the suffering and destruction described in the news.

The next day I saw vibrant community of Verdelia in action when I explored the town. Conversations with local inhabitants revealed stories of unity and cooperation. When I visited the market I saw a lively exchange of goods and cultures. Farmers from the countryside traded their fresh produce for essentials like cotton clothes. For example, one farmer swapped a bushel of vegetables for finely woven cotton garments made by local artisans. This not only fulfilled practical needs but also encouraged cultural exchange. I saw a spice merchant trading spices with a local baker, who shared baking techniques from their culture. Nearby artisans, who worked together, blended various craft techniques and styles. These interactions showed the town's spirit of collaboration.

I said to myelf, "Verdelia truly is a marvel of cooperation."

Returning to the retreat under the glow of solar lanterns, I shared my thoughts with Dad. I said, "Imagine if countries worked together like the people here in Verdelia. Instead of wars, they could collaborate for the well-being of everyone and the planet. This would help prevent the environmental damage and human suffering we read about." Dad nodded in agreement.

As we enjoyed another eco-friendly dinner, the idea of global unity felt more real. The world could benefit greatly from peace and cooperation, just like the way we have seen the community interacting in the bustling market of Verdelia.

Chapter 4
Harmony
with Nature

The following day my parents and I explored through the vibrant markets of Verdelia. My eyes widened at the kaleidoscope of colours and the bustling energy of local vendors. My eyes darted from one vendor to another. The diverse array of products sparked my curiosity.

I asked, "Mom, Dad! How does buying anything from this market make any difference?"

Mom pointed to a stall with handmade crafts and said, "Sam, responsible consumption means choosing products that are kind to the environment. Take these crafts, for example. They're made by local artisans. By buying these we are able to support the livelihoods of these artisans and help to keep the environment unpolluted."

Dad chimed in as he pointed toward a display of fruits and vegetables. He added, "Look at these fresh produce. They're locally sourced which means they did not travel long distances to reach us. It's better for the environment and it supports local farmers."

We strolled further. I noticed a shop with a variety of goods, some with excessive packaging and some with less. I asked, "Why are some things packaged so much and others aren't?"

Mom explained, "Good observation, Sam. Excessive packaging can be harmful to the environment. When we choose products with minimal packaging, we reduce waste. It's about being mindful of the impact our choices have on the planet."

Pointing to a sign that read 'Eco-Friendly Products' my Dad said, "Sam, see that? Some shops are committed to selling items that are environment friendly. Supporting such businesses encourages others to adopt sustainable practices too."

I nodded. Seeking clarification, I asked, "So, it's not just about what we buy but also where we buy it from?"

My parents smiled in agreement as they echoed, "Exactly, Sam. Every purchase is a vote for a better world. By supporting local, sustainable and eco-friendly products we contribute to a healthier planet and a thriving community."

As we continued exploring the market, my Dad shared additional insights. He said, "Sam, did you notice that some products are made from recycled materials? When we buy these, we give a second life to materials that might otherwise become waste."

My eyes widened with realization. I exclaimed, "So, it's like helping the planet in more ways than one!"

Mom nodded and said, "Absolutely, Sam. Responsible consumption is a powerful tool for positive change. It's not just about what we get, it's about the impact our choices have on the world around us."

Later as we headed back to the Whispering Pines Retreat, Dad continued sharing more of his wisdom. He continued, "You know, when Grandma used to cook, everything came from our fields or backyard. Rice and lentils from our paddy fields. Vegetables from our backyard. Even the water we used to rinse rice and lentils was served to plants. It's like we were living sustainably without even realizing it."

My parents smiled, realizing the profound impact of these practices. My Mom said, "Exactly, Sam. In the past, people often lived in harmony with nature. We can learn a lot from those practices like using biodegradable materials and turning kitchen scraps into compost. It's a wonderful way to care for the Earth and create a more sustainable future."

As we meandered through the bustling markets of Verdelia, we stumbled upon a stall showcasing an array of colourful bags. I picked one up and noticed a tag that read "Eco-Friendly Bags - Made from Recycled Plastic Bottles."

Curiosity lit up my eyes as I turned to my parents. I asked,"How can bags be made from recycled plastic bottles?"

With a smile, Dad explained, "Well, Sam, instead of letting plastic bottles end up in landfills, they are collected, cleaned and transformed into the material used to create these bags. It's a way of giving a second life to materials that would otherwise harm the environment."

I nodded my head in understanding, examining the bag more closely. I said,"That's really cool! Are there other things made from recycled materials?"

Mom pointed towards a nearby shop that showcased colourful stationery and said, "Absolutely, Sam! Take those notebooks, for instance. The paper they're made from comes from recycled materials, often old newspapers and cardboard. It reduces the need to cut down more trees."

As we continued exploring, my attention was drawn to a display of vibrant clothing. Dad picked up a shirt and remarked, "This shirt is made from recycled polyester, which comes from reused plastic bottles. It's a fantastic way to reduce the environmental impact of clothing production."

Walking further we encountered a variety of items made from recycled materials. From home decor to kitchenware, the market showcased the creativity and innovation that arises when materials are repurposed.

My Mom added, "By choosing products made from recycled materials, we're not only reducing waste but also supporting a more sustainable way of living. It's like giving a second chance to things that might otherwise end up as trash."

I couldn't help but appreciate the ingenuity behind these products. It was an example of how responsible consumption and recycling could make a positive impact on the environment, turning ordinary items into eco-friendly treasures.

As the evening sun dipped below the hills of Verdelia, we relaxed in the cozy ambience of Whispering Pines Retreat. The aroma of locally brewed coffee filled the air. My eyes, however, were drawn to a painting adorning the hotel room.

The painting depicted a dolphin navigating through turbulent waters, marred by pollution.

Intrigued, I turned to my dad and asked "Dad, what makes our oceans and seas so polluted? And why is it affecting creatures like dolphins?"

Dad, sipping his coffee made from locally sourced beans, welcomed the opportunity for a meaningful conversation. He said, "Well Sam,the pollution in oceans and seas comes from various sources. One major contributor is plastic waste. When people use plastic products carelessly, they often end up in water bodies, posing a threat to marine life."

My eyes widened as I processed this information. I asked, "So, plastic is harming dolphins?"

Dad nodded. "Exactly. Dolphins and other marine creatures can mistake plastic for food, leading to ingestion and harm. The pollution also affects their habitats and can disrupt entire ecosystems."

Pointing to the painting, I asked, "What else causes pollution in the oceans?"

Dad continued, "Apart from plastic, industrial discharges, oil spills and agricultural runoff are significant contributors. When factories release untreated waste into water bodies, it can harm aquatic life. Similarly, oil spills and runoff from farms introduce harmful substances into the oceans, creating a challenging environment for marine species."

With more awareness I asked, "What can we do to help, Dad?"

Appreciating my concern Dad smiled and said,"We can make conscious choices in our daily lives. For instance, using fewer single-use plastics, properly disposing waste and supporting initiatives that focus on cleaning and protecting our oceans. Additionally, choosing products made sustainably, like the ones we had seen in the market, is a step towards reducing our environmental impact."

As we continued our conversation, I was absorbed in the importance of responsible living and its impact on the planet. The painting, once a mere decoration, now served as a poignant reminder of the delicate balance between human actions and the well-being of Earth's diverse ecosystems. The evening unfolded with a newfound appreciation for the interconnectedness of all living beings and the role each person plays in preserving the beauty of the oceans and seas.

Chapter 5
The Green DataCenter

The day took an unexpected turn as I and my parents prepared to visit the local museum the next morning. My dad received an urgent call from the office. The plans for the museum visit had to be put on hold.

I was familiar with my Dad's ability to seamlessly blend work and family time. So, I tried to find solace in my Rubik's Cube, and waited for the call to conclude.

As I tried engaging myself in my puzzle, I observed my Dad. When the conversation shifted to emails and documents, I couldn't help but grow curious about the contents of the laptop screen. Impatience nudged me to move from the comfort of the sofa to stand behind Dad. I wondered how long this work endeavour would delay our museum plans.

To my surprise, I noticed something different in my Dad's email signature. There were no JPG files with the company logo. Puzzled, I questioned, "Dad, where's the company logo in your email signature? Did something happen to the files?"

Dad, still typing away, smiled at my inquisitiveness. He said, "No, Sam, nothing happened. I made a conscious decision not to include the company logo in my emails. You see, every time we send an email with attachments like logos or images, it contributes to more data being transmitted and processed. This in turn, increases energy consumption and carbon emissions."

My confusion still lingered, prompting my Dad to elaborate. He added, "Attaching files to emails requires servers to work more. These servers are powered by electricity, which may not be from sustainable sources. So, to align with our company's commitment to environmental responsibility and the concept of a green data center, I decided not to include the logo in my email signature."

I asked, "But how can we share logos or images without attaching them?"

Dad explained, "There are alternatives, Sam. Instead of attaching files directly, we can provide links to where the images are hosted online. This way, the recipient can view the image by clicking the link without increasing the data load in the email. It's a small change, but collectively, it can make a difference in reducing our environmental footprint."

Absorbing this new knowledge I nodded thoughtfully. "So, even in emails, we can do something to help the environment?"

My dad grinned. He said, "Absolutely, Sam. It's about making conscious choices in every aspect of our lives, even in seemingly small things like email signatures. If everyone does their bit, it adds up to a significant positive impact on the environment."

As the email was finally sent, I and my dad left the room, leaving behind the laptop screen that now reflected not just a message but a conscious decision to minimize environmental impact.

Chapter 6
Recycled Materials and the Museum

As we entered the museum, my eyes widened at the vibrant display of crafts. Local artisans had beautifully crafted products from recycled materials, showcasing the artistry born from sustainable practices. Intricate sculptures made from discarded metal, colourful rugs woven from recycled fabrics and artistic installations using repurposed materials adorned the museum floors.

My Mom explained, "Sam, these creations are not just beautiful. They also tell a story of sustainability and community ingenuity. By using recycled materials, these artisans contribute to reducing waste and promoting environmental awareness."

As we explored further, I was captivated by a section dedicated to indigenous ways of living in harmony with nature. Displays highlighted traditional practices such as the practise of organic farming, harvesting rainwater and harnessing renewable energy sources like solar and wind.

One exhibit particularly caught my attention. An interactive display demonstrating how communities reduced their carbon footprint by relying on locally sourced materials and renewable energy. I couldn't help but be inspired by the innovative approaches these communities had adopted.

As I wandered through the museum, my attention was suddenly drawn to a bustling stall tucked away in a corner. At the first glance, it seemed like an ordinary display, but upon closer inspection, I noticed a group of artisans meticulously crafting miniature wind turbines. These small wonders were ingeniously designed to harness the power of the wind, providing sustainable energy to light bulbs for shorter durations.

Intrigued by the process, I approached the stall and struck up a conversation with one of the artisans. I learned that these mini wind turbines were constructed using locally sourced materials such as bamboo, recycled metal parts and lightweight fabrics. The artisans explained how they carefully assembled each turbine by hand that ensured efficiency and durability.

The significance of these turbines became apparent as the artisan shared stories of their impact in Verdelia. In this quaint town nestled amidst green hills, many households relied on these mini wind turbines to illuminate their balconies during the evenings. Here, children could be seen engrossed in their studies under the gentle glow of lights powered by the eco-friendly wind turbines, while elders and senior citizens gathered together to chat amiably over cups of tea and organic snacks.

I exclaimed, "Organic Snacks!"

It was no wonder that the answer to it was also present inside the museum. In one exhibit, we found a demonstration of how local ingredients sourced from organic farms are transformed into delicious snacks.

A knowledgeable guide explained the process that highlighted the importance of using fresh and pesticide-free produce to ensure the snacks are not only healthy but also environmentally friendly.

The guide demonstrated how artisans skilfully prepare various snacks using traditional methods such as drying, roasting and fermentation. We witnessed the meticulous care taken in selecting the finest fruits, nuts and grains. I felt super excited to learn about the connection between sustainable agriculture and wholesome food production.

In another corner of the exhibit, we encountered a display showcasing innovative techniques for food preservation without the need for harmful chemicals or excessive packaging. From vegetable pickles to creating natural fruit preserves, the artisans demonstrated how simple yet effective methods can be employed to minimize food waste and promote sustainability.

We gained a newfound appreciation for the efforts put into promoting eco-friendly food practices within the local community. I was excited to discover how the local community had realized that sustainability extends beyond just materials and energy usage but also encompasses the way we nourish ourselves and interact with the environment through food choices.

ENTRY
CRAFT SECT
YOU CAN BE RESPONSIBLE AND FASHIONABLE TOO
RECYCLING FABRIC DEMO
SUSTAINABLE FASHION
RETHINK FASHION
LET FOOD BE THY MEDICINE AND MEDICINE BE THY FOOD
TEA (LOCAL)
ORGANIC TEA & SNACK
DEMO
SNACKS
DRINKS

Chapter 7
ESG T shirts

Next day as the golden rays of the morning sun danced across the azure canvas of the sky, I and my parents got ready to embrace a day filled with exploration and discovery. We stepped out into the beautiful streets of Verdelia. The weather was perfect. Tufts of white clouds floated lazily in the endless sky.

As we strolled through the vibrant streets of Verdelia, our eyes were drawn to the array of local stores lining the cobblestone pathways. Among them, a quaint garment store caught our attention. Its window displayed 'ESG' emboldened T-shirts.

Intrigued by the display, we stepped inside the store. We were greeted by racks of eco-friendly apparel. As we browsed through the selection, we came across an informational panel that introduced me to a new acronym called ESG.

As my curious gaze lingered on the bold ESG emblazoned T-shirts, my dad crouched down to my level. With a warm smile, he began, "Hey Sam, have you ever heard of ESG before? It stands for 'Environmental', 'Social' and 'Governance' ,but let's break it down a bit more when we go back to the retreat."

After purchasing two T-shirts emblazoned with the bold ESG print, we decided to explore more of Verdelia. The storekeeper had suggested visiting a nearby school renowned for its unique approach to education and sustainability and curiosity led us there.

Nestled amidst lush greenery, Verdelia Eco Academy stood as a beacon of modern education intertwined with a deep respect for nature. Alongside conventional subjects like Maths, English, Science, History and Geography the students were taught a subject uniquely named 'EarthSense'. This curriculum delved into topics like sustainability, environmental stewardship and the interconnectedness of ecosystems.

As we toured the school grounds, one feature that stood out was the expansive farmland surrounding the campus. Here, students cultivated grains and vegetables as part of their hands-on learning. What fascinated me the most was the practice of using the produce to cook meals right there in the school's kitchen. The students worked in teams to prepare steaming and hearty meals, which they shared in a common dining area.

We were lucky enough to join them for lunch that day. The dining area buzzed with laughter and chatter as students passed around bowls of steaming lentils, fragrant rice, fresh salads and homemade bread. I watched in amazement as the children enjoyed their food with a sense of accomplishment and pride, knowing they had been part of the entire process—from planting the seeds to harvesting and cooking.

As we explored further, I discovered another unique trait of Verdelia Eco Academy. After school hours, students were actively engaged in cleaning the school's toilets and washrooms. While initially surprised, I quickly realized the beauty of this practice. It instilled a sense of responsibility and humility among the students, teaching them the dignity of labour and the importance of maintaining shared spaces.

As we strolled back home Dad said, "Teaching the dignity of labour and the importance of maintaining shared spaces will go a long way in making these students responsible global citizens".

CAFE
erdelia
HOTEL
Love Earth Fashions
EVERY CHOICE YOU MAKE MATTERS
ESG Collections
FASHION FOR
EVERY SEASON

Chapter 8
Global Warming

As the evening unfolded and raindrops delicately tapped on the windowpanes, my entire family gathered in the cozy confines of the hotel room. Beyond the glass, Verdelia transformed into a world of pristine nature. We watched as the blades of grass and leaves got drenched and glistened with the heavy downpour. The air outside carried the unique scent of wet earth.

Choosing the warmth of the indoors we decided to watch a movie. Our pick was ' Lasting Echo of Harmony'. It was an epic tale that unfolded against the backdrop of catastrophic climate events. Outside, the rain intensified.

As the movie played, my attention shifted between the unfolding plot and the rain-soaked world outside. The scenes depicted a world in turmoil, with extreme weather events and a planet thrown into chaos. I turned to my parents and asked, "Dad, Mom, is this movie a possibility? Could the Earth really face such catastrophic events?" My eyes reflected a mix of curiosity and concern.

Dad nodded and said, "Well, Sam, the movie does highlight a real issue of climate change. Human activities such as burning fossil fuels and deforestation, releasing greenhouse gases, trapping heat in the atmosphere cause global warming."

I absorbed this information and further queried, "How does global warming impact the world?"

This time Mom chimed in as she said, "Global warming leads to rising temperatures, which, in turn, cause melting ice caps and glaciers. This results in sea-level rise, posing a threat to lowlands and coastal cities. The increased frequency and intensity of extreme weather events such as hurricanes and floods are also linked to climate change."

The rain outside seemed to echo the urgency in my question. Dad continued, "Human interventions such as excessive carbon emissions and the destruction of natural habitats accelerate these changes. It's crucial for us to adopt sustainable practices. We need to reduce our carbon footprint and work towards mitigating the impact of climate change."

I contemplated the relation between human actions and the well-being of the planet.

While sleeping that night I remembered that my Dad had forgotten to explain me all about ESG as he had mentioned the other day. I thought that I would wait for a day or two before asking him all about it.

"THE GREATEST THREAT TO OUR PLANET IS THE BELIEF THAT SOMEONE ELSE WILL SAVE IT" - Robert Swan

Chapter 9
ESG Revisited

Next day as I and my dad were exploring the city park in the afternoon, the lush greenery and the gentle hum of the city were suddenly interrupted when we heard a squabble nearby. We followed the sound and found a policeman engaged in a heated argument with a biker.

Drawn in by the commotion, we approached cautiously. While trying to understand the cause of the dispute it quickly became apparent that the altercation stemmed from a disagreement over the biker's disregard for following emission rules while riding his two-wheeler.

The policeman, with a furrowed brow and stern demeanour, emphasized the importance of adhering to emission regulations to protect air quality and public health. The biker looked visibly frustrated. He argued that the rules were overly restrictive and hindered his enjoyment of riding.

As we continued to observe the altercation between the policeman and the biker, I asked, "Hey, Dad. What causes emission?"

Dad quipped, "The fuel and non-adherence to emission control measures."

I looked at the passing trucks on the nearby road and asked, "How does fuel make the trucks emit things?"

Dad crouched down to my eye level and explained, "Alright, Sam. Inside the trucks, there are engines that need fuel to work. The trucks upon burning this fuel releases gases into the air. Some of these gases such as carbon dioxide and other pollutants contribute to what we call emissions."

I frowned, starting to grasp the concept. I asked,"So, it's like when we burn wood in the fireplace, and there's smoke?"

My Dad affirmed, "Exactly! Just like burning wood releases smoke, burning fuel in trucks releases gases into the air. Now, imagine if all those trucks in the company switched to electric ones. Instead of burning fuel, they would use batteries to power electric motors."

My eyes widened with curiosity. I asked, "Batteries? Like the ones in my toys?"

My Dad explained, "Exactly, Sam! Instead of burning fuel, these trucks would run on electricity stored in large batteries. It's a cleaner way to move things around because there's no burning involved. No smoke, no harmful emissions."

As Dad finished explaining about emissions, he paused for a moment. The argument between the policeman and the biker had started to draw a small crowd.

Dad smiled thoughtfully and said, "You know, Sam, this reminds me of something I promised to explain to you a while ago. We started talking about ESG. It's something that fits perfectly with what's happening here."

I tilted my head, intrigued as Dad said, "Well, ESG stands for Environmental, Social, and Governance. It's a way people and companies make sure they're doing the right thing for the planet, for others and for themselves. Let me explain it in three parts."

He gestured to the biker and said, "The argument you see here is all about the 'E' in ESG that emphasises upon environmental responsibility. It's about making choices that protect the air, water and land around us. When people follow emission rules, like the policeman is trying to enforce, they're helping reduce pollution and slow down climate change. It's like making sure we don't hurt the earth while we enjoy the things it gives us."

I nodded, looking at the biker's frowning face and asked, "So, the biker not following the rules is bad for the environment? "

Dad said, "Exactly! That's why the policeman is upset. He's not just trying to make life hard for the biker; he's thinking about everyone who breathes this air."

Pointing at the people gathered around us, Dad continued, "Now, the 'S' stands for Social. It's about how we treat each other and how our actions affect society. For example, when the biker ignores the rules, he's not just hurting the environment but also other people's health. A big part of ESG is thinking about how our choices impact others and making sure we act fairly and responsibly."

I glanced at the small group of onlookers, some covering their noses as a truck rumbled by, belching smoke. I asked, "So, it's like being nice to others by following the rules? "

Dad said, "Exactly. It's about thinking beyond yourself."

Next pointing to the policeman, Dad said, "And the 'G' stands for Governance. That's about the rules, laws and systems that help people and companies do the right thing. The policeman here is part of that governance. He's making sure the rules are followed so everyone can enjoy a healthier and safer life."

I stared at the policeman, suddenly seeing him in a different light. I said, "So, ESG is like making sure everyone plays fair for the earth, for people and for the rules?"

Dad beamed in as he said, "Exactly, Sam! It's a way of making the world better and ensuring that we leave it in good shape for you and others like you."

I looked back at the biker and said, "I think I get it now, Dad. It's about doing the right thing even when it's hard."

Dad ruffled my hair as he said, "You've got it, Sam. And if you can remember this lesson, you'll be on your way to making a big difference in the world someday."

I continued and asked,"Hey Dad! Do you think it's really possible to have a completely emission free world?"

Dad paused, considering the question thoughtfully. He replied, "Well, Sam. It's a complex issue. While achieving a completely emission free world may seem like a daunting task, it's important to recognize that every small step toward reducing emissions can make a significant difference."

I nodded. Still seemed skeptical I asked, "But Dad, with so many cars on the road and factories pumping out smoke, isn't it unrealistic to think we can eliminate all emissions?"

Understanding my concern Dad smiled and said, "You're right, Sam. It's not realistic to expect zero emissions overnight. That's where the concept of scope 1, 2, and 3 emissions comes into play."

I asked, "Scope 1, 2, and 3 emissions?"

Dad explained, "Scope 1 emissions are direct emissions that occur from sources that are owned or controlled by a company. For example, direct emissions from a manufacturing company would fall under scope 1."

I nodded and said, "Ah, I see. So, what about scope 2 and 3 emissions?"

Dad continued, "Scope 2 emissions are indirect emissions from the generation of electricity, heating or cooling that a company consumes."

I asked, "Are you forgetting scope 3 emissions?"

Dad grinned and replied,"No my boy. Scope 3 emissions are indirect emissions that occur as a result of a company's activities, but are not directly owned or controlled by the company itself. This could include emissions from the supply chain, transportation or disposal of products."

And then he looked at my confused and yet inquisitive eyes.

He smiled warmly and dived into a more detailed explanation as he said, "Alright, Sam, let's break it down. Imagine a clothing brand, like the ones we see in stores. Now, when we talk about emissions, it's not just about what happens in the factory where the clothes are made. There's a whole journey the clothes take from production to when we wear them and even beyond."

I listened intently and asked, "So, what are scope 3 emissions then?"

Dad explained, "Well, scope 3 emissions are kind of like the hidden emissions that come from all the other stuff that happens along the way. For instance, think about the trucks and vans that carry the clothes from factories to the stores. Those vehicles produce emissions as they travel and add to the overall impact of the clothing brand."

I nodded, starting to grasp the concept and asked, "But what else counts as scope 3 emissions?"

My Dad replied, "Good question. There's also the energy used to make the materials that go into the clothes, like growing cotton or making synthetic fibers. Then, once we have the clothes, there's the energy we use to wash and dry them at home. And even after we're done with them, when clothes end up in a landfill, they can produce greenhouse gases as they break down."

My eyes widened as I considered the various ways emissions could be generated throughout the lifecycle of clothing. I asked, "Can there still be a lot of emissions even if a company makes their factories eco-friendly?"

My Dad verified, "Exactly! That's why it's important for companies to look beyond just their own operations and consider all the different ways their products impact the environment. By understanding and addressing scope 1, 2 and 3 emissions they can work towards reducing their overall carbon footprint and making a positive difference."

I summarised, "So, by understanding and addressing scope 1, 2, and 3 emissions, companies and individuals can take meaningful steps to reduce their overall carbon footprint."

My dad continued, "Exactly! It's all about taking responsibility for our actions and working together to create a more sustainable future, one step at a time."

Verdelia City Park

Chapter 10
Vanquishing
Emission

The following afternoon, as the sun lazily dipped behind the hills, I and my parents decided to spend a quiet moment indoors after a delightful lunch at the Whispering Pines Retreat.

Seated in the cozy sofa of the hotel room I dozed off into a brief nap. In my dream, I found myself in a world where emissions appeared as ominous clouds threatening to shroud the beauty of the environment. Fueled by a newfound understanding of ESG and Emissions I stood tall like a guardian, ready to confront the looming threat.

As the dark emissions cloud attempted to engulf the landscape, I countered it with beams of renewable energy. Each burst of sustainable power dispelled the ominous clouds to reveal a cleaner and brighter world. In my dream I felt the weight of responsibility and the impact of informed choices on the environment.

When I woke from my nap, I carried the vivid dream with me. I recalled how it is essential to encourage businesses to make eco-friendly choices in their energy consumption.

As the sun dipped further, I felt a sense of empowerment to champion a cleaner, greener future.

What
we save
saves us

Chapter 11
Eco Conscious Farm

Next day my family decided to embark on a day trip to a nearby eco conscious farm. My parents saw this as an opportunity to not only enjoy the beauty of nature but also to impart valuable lessons about sustainability to their curious son.

As we set out on the scenic drive, my parents began explaining the concept of an eco-conscious farm. My Mom said,"Sam, an eco-conscious farm is a place that prioritizes environment friendly and sustainable practices. They use methods that minimize harm to the environment, like organic farming, responsible water management and renewable energy sources."

With curiosity gleaming in my eyes, I asked, "Why are we visiting the farm?"

Mom smiled and said, "Great question, Sam! We're going to learn about where our food comes from and how the choices we make impact the environment. It's a chance to see firsthand how a farm can be both productive and eco-friendly."

Upon arriving at the eco-conscious farm we were greeted by green fields, the scent of blooming flowers and a serene ambience. As we explored the farm, I kept gazing at the rows of vegetables, the orchards and the overall harmony between agriculture and nature.

After engaging with the farmers, I and my family learned about sustainable farming practices. We also understood the importance of biodiversity. Gesturing toward the buzzing beehives and the composting area, my Dad explained, "Sam, the choices we make about the food we buy and eat have an impact beyond just what's on our plate. It involves how the food is grown, transported and even packaged. All these factors contribute to the farm's Scope 3 emissions."

Surrounded by the sights and sounds of the eco-conscious farm I began to connect the dots. Our family discussion delved into responsible sourcing, the carbon footprint associated with transportation and the importance of supporting local and sustainable agriculture.

The visit to the eco-conscious farm transformed into a day of immersive learning for us. As we left the farm, I carried with me not just memories of a beautiful day but a deeper understanding of how choices, even those related to food can impact our environment.

We don't have
to sacrifice a
strong economy
for a healthy
environment.
— Donnie Wears
VERDELIA'S VERY OWN
ECO-CONCIOUS FARM. ESTD: 2015

Chapter 12
The Return

The following day I woke up and it took some time for me to understand that finally, the day to return back home had arrived. I was a little sad as I realized that our stay at the eco-conscious Whispering Pines Retreat had come to an end.

The serene surroundings and eco-friendly practices of the retreat had become familiar and comforting during our stay. However, the time had come to bid farewell and head to the airport for our journey back home.

The hotel staff warmly waved goodbye. We left the Whispering Pines with a sense of appreciation for the retreat's commitment to environmental responsibility.

By now I was accustomed to viewing the world through the lens of sustainability. At the airport I couldn't help but wonder about the airport's environmental efforts. As we stood in line for security checks, I turned to my parents with a barrage of questions.

I asked, "Mom, Dad, airports are huge! How do they manage their emissions? Are they doing anything to be more environment friendly?"

Mom chuckled and said, "Good observations, Sam! Airports indeed have a significant impact towards environment pollution. However steps are being taken to mitigate it. For instance, some airports invest in renewable energy sources such as solar panels to power their facilities. This helps reduce reliance on traditional energy sources that contribute to carbon emissions."

As we walked through the bustling terminal, I noticed electric buses transporting passengers. I asked, "Dad, what about those electric buses? Are they better for the environment?"

Dad nodded and said, "Exactly, Sam. Electric ground vehicles like passenger shuttles help cut down on emissions compared to traditional fuel-powered vehicles. It's a small but impactful step in making airport operations more sustainable."

While waiting at the gate I continued my exploration of airport sustainability. I asked, "How can airports reduce waste? There's so much going on here."

My Mom explained, "Airports can implement robust recycling programs and minimize use of plastics. Many are transitioning to recyclable materials for in-flight meal packing. This reduces the environmental impact of waste generated during travel."

Once inside plane, I peered through the window and asked, "Are airplanes themselves getting more eco-friendly?"

Dad shared insights and replied, "Yes, Sam. Airlines are investing in modern aircraft with advanced fuel-efficient technologies. Newer planes burn less fuel per passenger. This is a significant step toward making air travel more environment friendly."

During the flight, I pondered on the efforts required for sustainable air travel. As we landed back at our home airport I thought how the journey from the eco-conscious retreat to the airport had not only been a physical voyage but a learning experience for me, solidifying my understanding of the real-world efforts to reduce emissions in aviation and transportation.

After off-boarding the flight we collected our luggage and stepped out of the airport. We took a cab to take us home. On the way, my Dad decided to make a quick stop at an ATM to withdraw some cash.

The cab slowed down as my Dad stepped out. I couldn't resist turning to my Mom and asked,"Mom, do banks contribute to emissions too? I mean there seems to be a connection to the environment anywhere and everywhere we go."

Seizing the teachable moment, my Mom smiled and said, "Absolutely, Sam. Banks play a crucial role in what is known as sustainable finance. It's about how financial institutions make decisions that not only consider profit but also the impact on the environment and society."

My curiosity piqued. I listened intently as my Mom continued, "For example, banks can choose to invest in projects and companies that follow eco-friendly practices such as renewable energy or sustainable agriculture. They can also promote green initiatives as they provide support to businesses that prioritize environmental and social responsibility."

My Dad, rejoining the cab with cash in hand, overheard us and chimed in, "Sam, even the way banks operate can make a difference. Some banks are embracing digital technologies to reduce the need for physical branches, cutting down on energy consumption and paper usage. Sustainable finance is about aligning financial decisions with environmental and social values."

Connecting the dots from our stay at the eco-conscious retreat to the airport and now to the bank, I nodded thoughtfully. I asked, "So, it's not just about where we stay or how we travel. Even where we keep our money matters for the environment?"

My Mom nodded, "Exactly, Sam. Every aspect of our lives, including how we manage our finances, can have an impact. By choosing banks and financial institutions that prioritize sustainability, we contribute to a more eco-friendly and responsible world."

As the cab continued its journey, my understanding of sustainability expanded once again. The concept of sustainable finance became another layer in my growing awareness of the relation between daily choices and their environmental consequences. The cab ride home became more than just a commute. It became a conversation about how even financial decisions can be a force for positive change in the world.

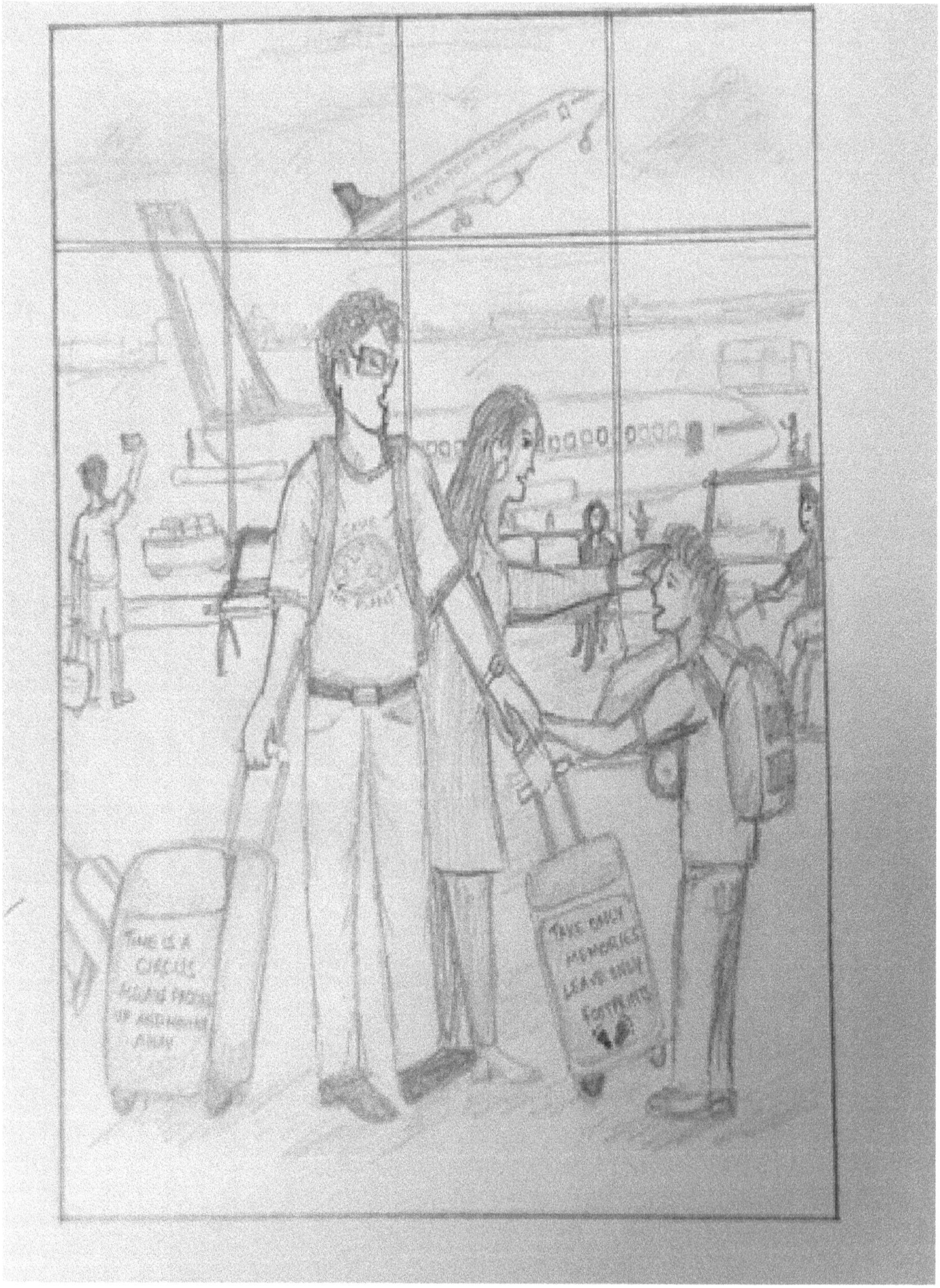
TIME IS A
TAKE ONLY
MEMORIES
LEAVE ONLY
FOOTPRINTS

Chapter 13
Back Home

Back home, the comforting aroma of a simple yet delicious meal filled the air as I and my family settled into the familiar surroundings of our own kitchen.

My mom, inspired by the sustainable practices we had witnessed at the Whispering Pines Retreat, decided to create a meal using the thoughtful gift we had received from the hotel staff. Fresh rice and vegetables sourced directly from local farmers.

The kitchen buzzed with activity as my mom carefully rinsed the vibrant vegetables that were cultivated in the fertile lands surrounding the retreat. The colours of the produce painted a vivid picture of the local harvest. Rich greens, vibrant reds and earthy browns.

With a practiced hand, she set the rice to cook. The comforting scent mingled with the freshness of the vegetables.

The vegetables sizzled in the pan and released a melody of enticing scents. My mom shared the story behind their ingredients. She said, "These vegetables, Sam, are a gift from the local farmers near the Whispering Pines Retreat. It's a wonderful way to support the community and enjoy produce that's not only fresh but also grown sustainably."

The dining table was soon adorned with a spread that mirrored the colours of the fields we had explored during our vacation. The rice, cooked to perfection, formed a bed for the vibrant medley of vegetables. The simplicity of the meal showcased the purity of the ingredients, allowing the natural flavours to shine.

As we sat down to enjoy the meal, my family felt connected to the journey we had experienced from the nature-friendly retreat to the airport and now to our own dining table. Every bite reminded us of the importance of living sustainably, showing how our choices not only mattered in the present but also supported local farmers and cared for the Earth.

The joy of the meal wasn't just about its delicious taste but about realizing that every ingredient had its own story. It reflected their efforts to support local communities and care for the environment. The kitchen became a special place again, filled with shared moments and thoughtful choices, where a simple meal represented the values of responsible living we had learned during our travels.

Chapter 14
The Gift

After the delightful lunch made from the locally sourced vegetables and rice, the atmosphere in my home shifted to a different kind of activity. The thoughtful act of gift-giving. Inspired by their experiences at the Whispering Pines Retreat, my parents had purchased a unique shirt for my cousin from the local artisan's market, a vibrant piece crafted with natural dyes.

As my family gathered around the table, my mom pulled out the neatly folded shirt. Its colours reflected the hues of the retreat's surroundings. My parents explained that the shirt was not only a stylish gift but also a sustainable one. It was produced using natural dyes instead of synthetic chemicals.

Eager to contribute, I took charge of the gift-wrapping process. The dining table transformed into a makeshift gift-wrapping station. As I carefully wrapped the shirt with colourful paper and twine, I thought at how this gift carried not only the essence of local craftsmanship but also a reflected commitment to eco-friendly practices.

My parents, observing my diligence, joined in the conversation. My Mom said, "Sam, the use of natural dyes in this shirt is a great example of sustainable fashion. Unlike conventional dyes that can harm the environment, natural dyes are derived from plants, fruits or even minerals. This makes them a more environment friendly choice."

With an air of pride I finished tying the twine around the neatly wrapped gift. I understood that sustainable choices extended beyond what we eat or where we stay. They also manifested in the products we buy and gift to others.

We decided to hand-deliver the gift to my cousin, who lived just two blocks away. As we walked through the neighborhood, the shirt, wrapped in eco-friendly packaging, symbolized a small but meaningful gesture of sharing the values we had embraced during our travels.

At my cousin's doorstep, we presented the gift with a smile, explaining the story behind the unique shirt. The day, which began with the memories of our eco-conscious journey, ended with the joy of sharing that newfound awareness with loved ones. The shirt, crafted by local artisans, became more than just clothing. It was a symbol of their dedication to sustainable living.

Chapter 15
The Dream

In the tranquil evening glow, as my family gathered around the television, a news segment caught our attention. A distressing incident in a local engineering college where a student had been subjected to ragging that ultimately leaded to his hospitalization. The sombre atmosphere in the room prompted me to ask a question that had been simmering in my mind.

With concern in my voice, I inquired, "Why can't students in colleges or schools contribute to a sustainable environment by being friendly and respectful? Why do some resort to unruly behavior?"

My parents turned off the television and invited me to sit with them. They explained that creating a sustainable environment goes beyond just ecological considerations. It also encompasses fostering a culture of respect, empathy and kindness.

My Dad said, "Sam, a sustainable environment isn't just about preserving nature. It's about building a society where everyone feels safe, respected and valued."

My Mom added, "It's crucial to cultivate an atmosphere that promotes positive interactions and discourages harmful practices like ragging in educational institutions, workplaces and communities."

Dad added, "Behaviours that harm others not only have immediate consequences but can also create a toxic environment that lingers. Sustainable living extends to how we treat one another with fairness, compassion and understanding. This principle applies not just in schools but in all aspects of life, including public and private offices and organizations."

Absorbing the message, I nodded thoughtfully and realized sustainability embraces the very essence of how people treat each other that fosters a sense of community and well-being.

As the evening continued, the family engaged in a heartfelt conversation about the importance of empathy and the need to promote a culture of inclusion. As the conversation progressed I understood that individual actions, whether in a college or a workplace, contribute to the overall health and resilience of the environment we collectively share. The news story, though distressing, became a catalyst for a meaningful discussion about the relation between environmental and social sustainability.

That night, as I entered the world of dreams, a poignant and enlightening story unfolded in my subconscious mind. A tale once shared with me by my Mom.

In a quaint village surrounded by hills and whispering pines, a revered old man was known for his wisdom. The villagers often turned to him to seek answers to life's problems. Inspired by the wisdom of his mom's words, a curious young boy, set out to challenge the old man's reputed sagacity.

The boy devised a plan, capturing a small sparrow and concealing it in his hands. Approaching the wise old man, he inquired, "Wise old man, can you tell what I have in my hands?"

The old man, keenly observant, replied confidently, "From all the small feathers clinging to your jacket and pants, it is plain to see it is a little bird you have cradled in your hands."

Undeterred, the boy pressed on, "Ah, that is so, but is the bird alive or dead?"

The old man paused. He rubbed his chin in contemplation. Instead of falling into the trap, he looked at the boy's eyes and responded, "Whether the bird is alive or dead is in your hands, my child. The choice is yours."

As I dreamt this familiar tale, I awoke with a profound realization. The story, once a lesson shared by my Mom, now resonated even more deeply. Just as the young boy held the destiny of the bird, individuals held the power to determine the fate of sustainability and the environment. The narrative crystallized in my mind. It emphasized the pivotal role each person plays in either nurturing or undermining the delicate balance of our planet.

The dream left an indelible mark on my consciousness, reinforcing the notion that sustainability is not an abstract concept but a tangible responsibility to be carried by every individual. The story, a cherished gift from my Mom, served as a poignant reminder that the power to create or disrupt harmony with nature lies within each of us.

Let all of us approach life with mindfulness, compassion and a commitment to safeguarding the WORLD and its ENVIRONMENT.